Library Day

BY *Anne Rockwell*

ILLUSTRATED BY *Lizzy Rockwell*

ALADDIN · New York · London · Toronto · Sydney · New Delhi

In memory of
Mrs. Mac and Kathy
and for
Mr. Miguel A. García-Colón of the
Byram Shubert Library, a branch of the Greenwich Library

On Saturday, I go to the new library with my father.

It's the first time we've been there together.

Before we go inside, we drop the books he borrowed through the slot.

I hear them thump in the bin when they land.

Children's Room

My father brings me to the children's room for story hour.

He tells me he will go to the grown-up shelves to look for a new book.

There are two boys and three girls sitting in a circle.

I sit next to a boy who has a green shirt on.

I've seen him at the playground.

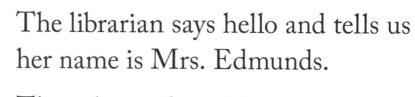

The librarian says hello and tells us her name is Mrs. Edmunds.

Then she reads us *The Three Sillies*.

After Mrs. Edmunds is done, she introduces Mr. Miguel.

He reads us a story from his homeland of Puerto Rico.

It's about a donkey named Señor Burro.

We all listen quietly, except when we laugh.

It's especially funny when Mr. Miguel goes,
"Hee-haw! Hee-haw!" as loud as he can.

When story hour is finished, the boy in the green shirt
tells me his name is Jack, and I tell him mine is Don.

Now we have time to look at all the cool things in the library.

I thought there were just books here.

But Jack shows me a shelf with movies and a rack with magazines in the corner.

I like the magazine about dogs, because there's an article in it about a puppy who looks just like our dog, Reggie, did when he was a puppy.

I also like a magazine about rabbits
and chickens and farm animals.

After I put the magazines back, I go to a low shelf filled with picture books.

I take a book with a tiger on the front.

Mr. Miguel shows me a book. He says, "It looks like you like books about animals. Maybe you'd like this one. The boy in the book has a snake for a pet."

I show him the book about a big red truck.

"I like this one too," I say.

"You can take them all home," Mr. Miguel says.

Next to the picture book bin there is a baby sitting on the floor with lots of books to read.

Except the baby is reading her book upside down.

She goes, "Goo-goo, gaa-baa, woo."

Then she turns the page, but her book is *still* upside down.

N. J. ALCORN

123

Jack has gone home, but I have time to explore.

Across the room, some big boys and girls are playing chess quietly.

A big boy is sitting at a computer.

Two girls are making bookmarks.

I look through the three books again, and then the librarian's helper puts a new book on the shelf.

It's about apples and pumpkins.

Hey! I like apples.

I like pumpkins.

So I bet I'll like this book!

Just then my father comes in to the children's room.

I ask him if I can take out these four books.

He says yes.

And then he says, "But you will need your own library card."

My own library card!

We walk to the front desk.

We hand our books to Mrs. Edmunds.

My father says that I would like my own card.

Mrs. Edmunds smiles and says, "I can see he's a real reader!"

I tell her my full name and where I live.

We wait a few minutes while lights on her machine go on and off as it rumbles.

"Here you are, Don," she says. She hands me a card with my own name written on the back!

Mrs. Edmunds scans the bar codes on my books with her little green light and reminds me to return them in two weeks.

Outside the door, there is a poster of a puppet show about the Gingerbread Man.

My father reads it to me and asks, "Would you like to go see that puppet show next Saturday?"

"I sure would," I say.

I take my father's hand as we cross the street and head home.

ALADDIN

An imprint of Simon & Schuster Children's Publishing Division

1230 Avenue of the Americas, New York, New York 10020

First Aladdin paperback edition January 2017

For information about special discounts for bulk purchases, please contact Simon & Schuster Special Sales at 1-866-506-1949 or business@simonandschuster.com.

The Simon & Schuster Speakers Bureau can bring authors to your live event. For more information or to book an event contact the Simon & Schuster Speakers Bureau at 1-866-248-3049 or visit our website at www.simonspeakers.com.

Designed by Jessica Handelman

The illustrations for this book were rendered in watercolor.

The text of this book was set in Caslon.

Manufactured in China 1016 SCP

10 9 8 7 6 5 4 3 2 1

Library of Congress Control Number 2015940058

ISBN 978-1-4814-2731-9 (hc)

ISBN 978-1-4814-2732-6 (pbk)

ISBN 978-1-4814-2733-3 (eBook)